PETER BOLLINGER

ALGERNON GRAEVES IS SCARY ENOUGH

LAURA GERINGER BOOKS
An Imprint of HarperCollinsPublishers

Library of Congress Cataloging-in-Publication Data

Bollinger, Peter.
   Algernon Graeves is scary enough / Peter Bollinger. — 1st ed.
      p.   cm.
   Summary: Algernon Graeves wants to wear the darkest, scariest Halloween costume
ever to go trick-or-treating and finally thinks of just the right thing.
   ISBN 0-06-052268-2 — ISBN 0-06-052269-0 (lib. bdg.)
   [1. Halloween—Fiction. 2. Costume—Fiction.] I. Title.
PZ7.B635927AI 2005   2003014175
[E]—dc22   CIP
                                                                  AC

Typography by Neil Swaab
1 2 3 4 5 6 7 8 9 10
❖
First Edition

for Zak

Deep in a dark, scary corner of his dark, scary attic, during the darkest, scariest month of the whole dark and scary year, Algernon Graeves was trying to think of the darkest, scariest, set-your-teeth-on-edgiest Halloween costume ever.

"A ghost!" thought Algernon Graeves. "Ghosts are scary."
So Algernon dressed up as a ghost.

But that wasn't scary enough.

"A skeleton!" thought Algernon Graeves.
"Skeletons are definitely scarier than ghosts."
So Algernon dressed up as a skeleton.

But that wasn't scary enough.

"How about a mummy!" thought Algernon Graeves. "Mummies are super scary." So Algernon dressed up as a mummy.

But that wasn't scary enough.

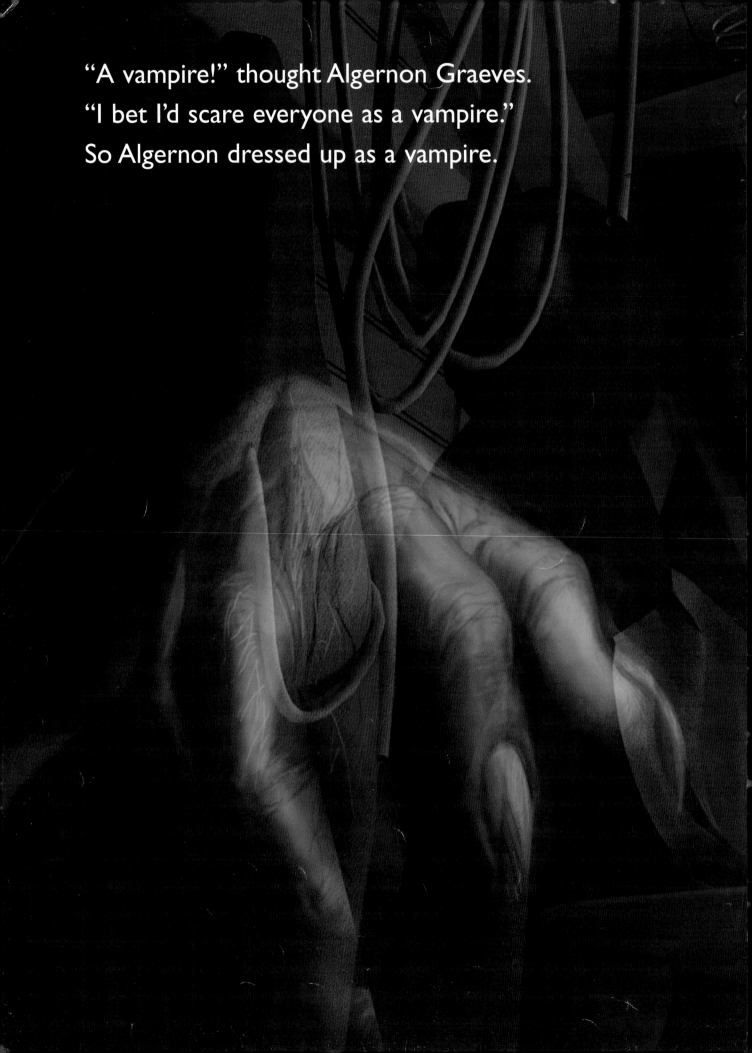

"A vampire!" thought Algernon Graeves.
"I bet I'd scare everyone as a vampire."
So Algernon dressed up as a vampire.

But that wasn't scary enough.

"I know!" thought Algernon Graeves. "A werewolf!"
So Algernon dressed up as a werewolf.

But that wasn't scary enough.

"I've got it now!" thought Algernon Graeves.
"Nothing is scarier than a zombie!"
So Algernon dressed up as a zombie.

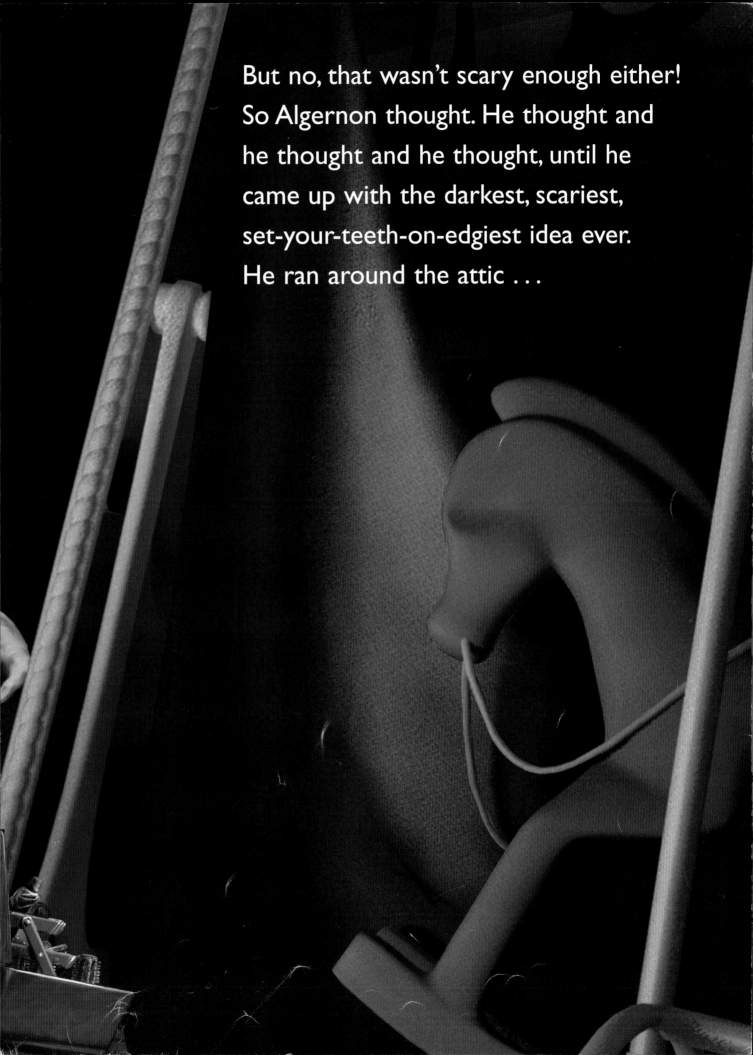

But no, that wasn't scary enough either!
So Algernon thought. He thought and
he thought and he thought, until he
came up with the darkest, scariest,
set-your-teeth-on-edgiest idea ever.
He ran around the attic . . .

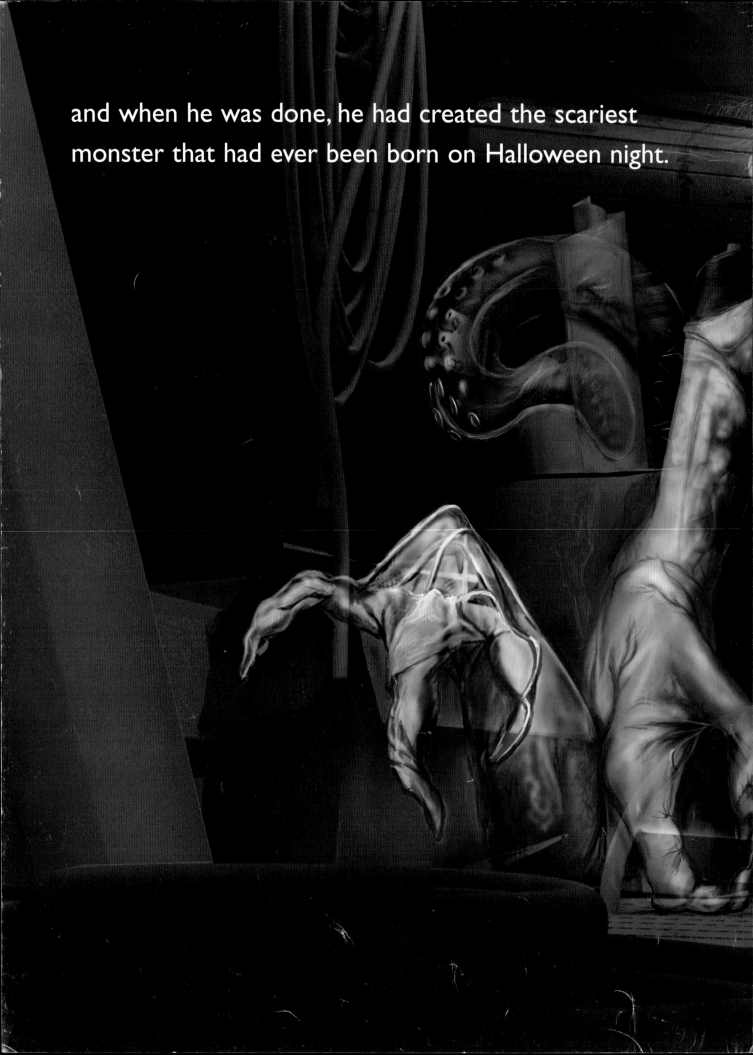

and when he was done, he had created the scariest monster that had ever been born on Halloween night.

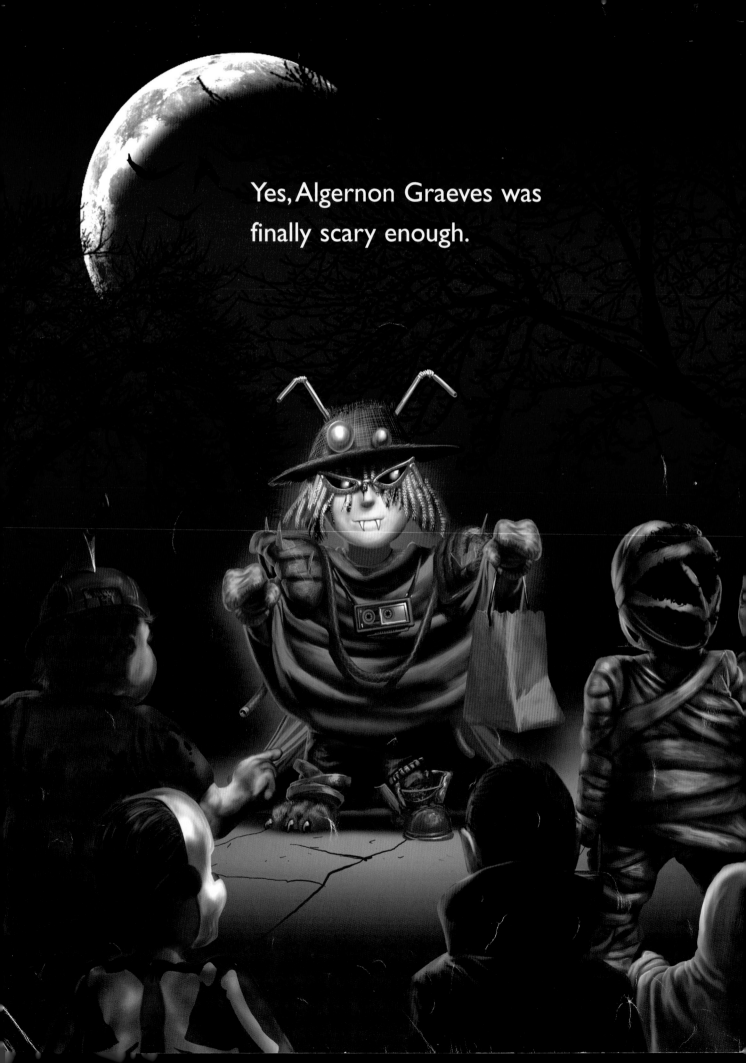

Yes, Algernon Graeves was
finally scary enough.